El Zorro y la Grulla

Una Fábula de Esopo

The Fox and the Crane

An Aesop's Fable

retold by Dawn Casey

illustrated by Jago

Spanish translation by Marta Belén Sáez Cabero

Fox started it. He invited Crane to dinner...
When Crane arrived at Fox's house she saw dishes
of every colour and kind lined the shelves.
Big ones, tall ones, short ones, small ones.
The table was set with two dishes. Two flat shallow dishes.

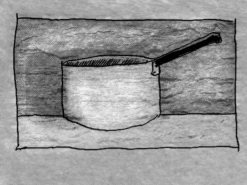

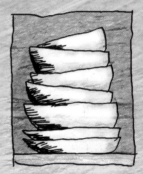

El Zorro empezó todo. Invitó a cenar a la Grulla…
Cuando la Grulla llegó a la casa del Zorro, vio platos y vasijas
de todo tipo y color alineados en las estanterías. Grandes, altos,
bajos, pequeños.
En la mesa había dos platos. Dos platos planos.

La Grulla dio un picotazo y tocó algo con su largo y delgado pico. Pero por mucho que lo intentó fue incapaz siquiera de tomar un solo sorbo de la sopa.

  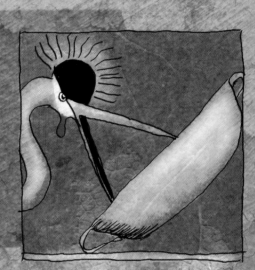

Crane pecked and she picked with her long thin beak. But no matter how hard she tried she could not get even a sip of the soup.

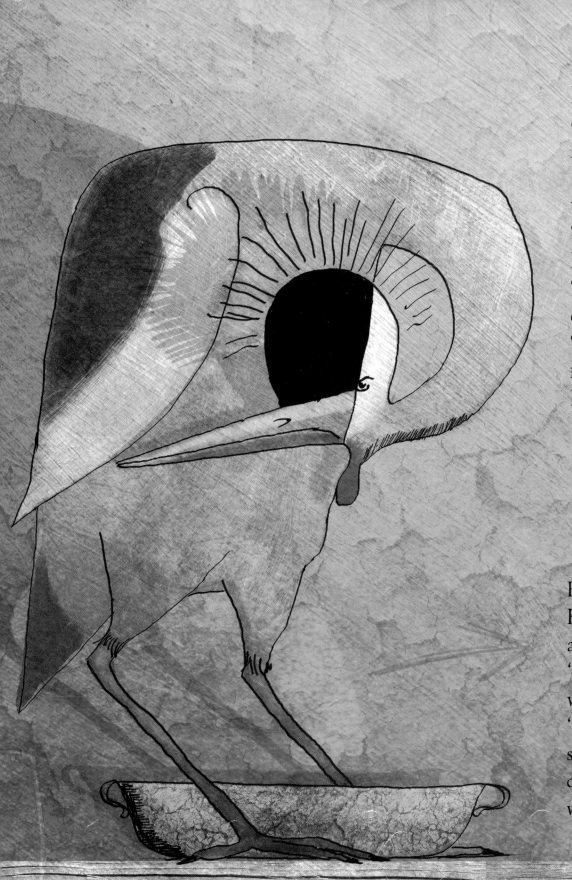

El Zorro se reía con disimulo mientras observaba los esfuerzos de la Grulla. Acercó la sopa a sus labios, y SORBO A SORBO, se la bebió toda a lengüetadas.
"¡Ahhhh, deliciosa!", dijo con sorna limpiándose los bigotes con la pata.
"Oh, Grulla, no ha tocado la sopa", dijo el Zorro con una sonrisilla.
"SIENTO que no le gustara", añadió mientras intentaba que no se le escapara una risotada.

Fox watched Crane struggling and sniggered. He lifted his own soup to his lips, and with a SIP, SLOP, SLURP he lapped it all up.
"Ahhhh, delicious!" he scoffed, wiping his whiskers with the back of his paw.
"Oh Crane, you haven't touched your soup," said Fox with a smirk. "I AM sorry you didn't like it," he added, trying not to snort with laughter.

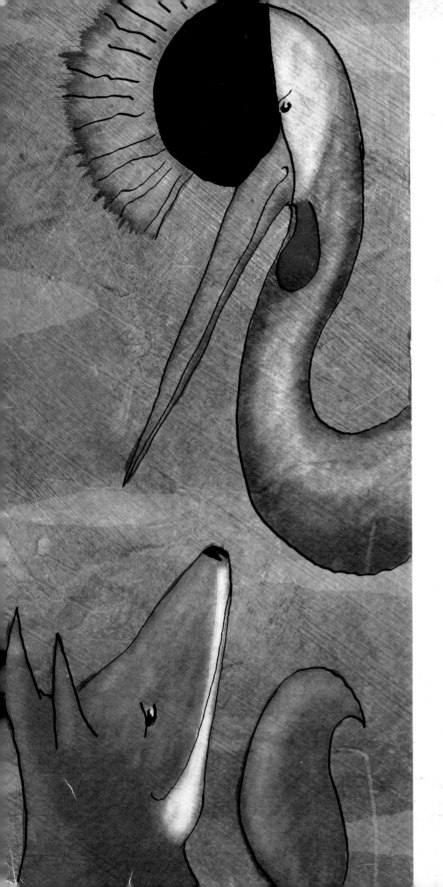

La Grulla no dijo nada. Miró la comida. Miró el plato. Miró al Zorro, y sonrió.

"Querido Zorro, gracias por su amabilidad", dijo la Grulla educadamente. "Por favor, permítame devolverle el favor. Venga a cenar a mi casa".

Cuando el Zorro llegó, la ventana estaba abierta. Un delicioso olor salía de ella. El Zorro levantó el hocico y olfateó. Se le hizo la boca agua. Le sonaron las tripas. Se relamió los labios.

Crane said nothing. She looked at the meal. She looked at the dish. She looked at Fox, and smiled.

"Dear Fox, thank you for your kindness," said Crane politely. "Please let me repay you – come to dinner at my house."

When Fox arrived the window was open. A delicious smell drifted out. Fox lifted his snout and sniffed. His mouth watered. His stomach rumbled. He licked his lips.

"Mi querido Zorro, entre", dijo la Grulla tendiendo su ala gentilmente.
El Zorro avanzó. Vio platos y vasijas de todo tipo y color alineados en las estanterías. Rojos, azules, viejos, nuevos.
En la mesa había dos vasijas.
Dos vasijas altas y estrechas.

"My dear Fox, do come in," said Crane, extending her wing graciously.
Fox pushed past. He saw dishes of every colour and kind lined the shelves.
Red ones, blue ones, old ones, new ones.
The table was set with two dishes.
Two tall narrow dishes.

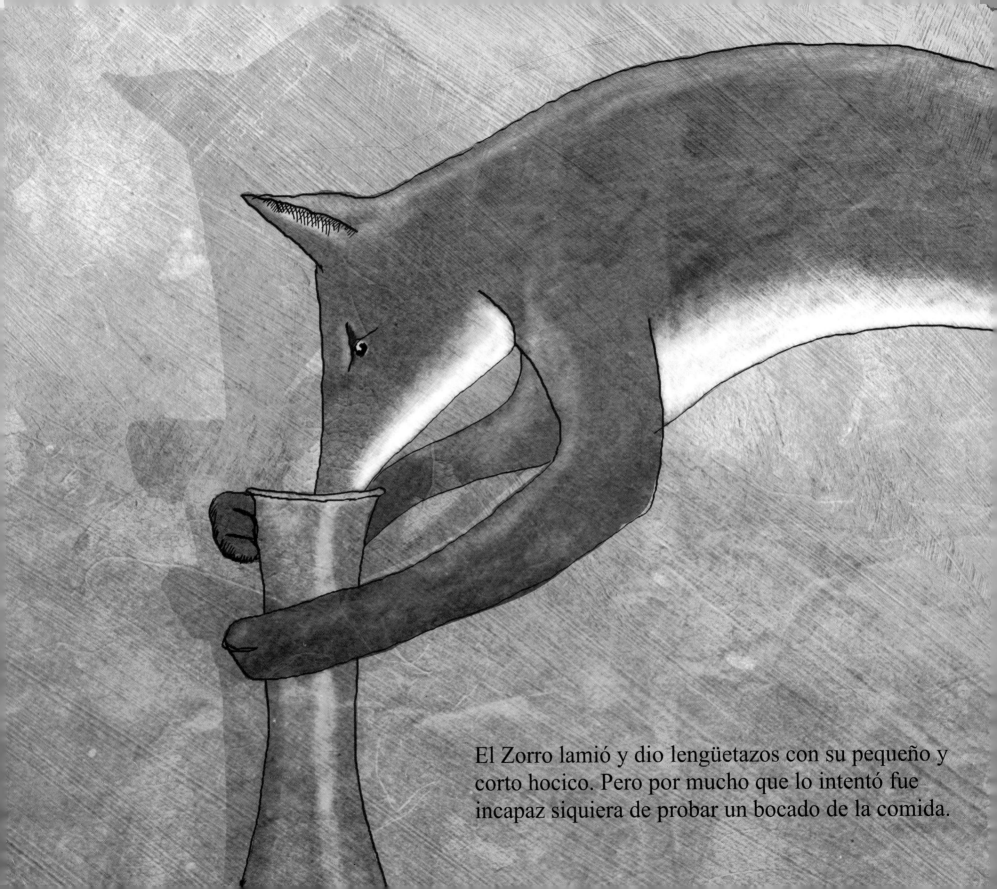

El Zorro lamió y dio lengüetazos con su pequeño y corto hocico. Pero por mucho que lo intentó fue incapaz siquiera de probar un bocado de la comida.

Fox licked and he lapped with his short little snout.
But no matter how hard he tried he could not
get even a mouthful of the meal.

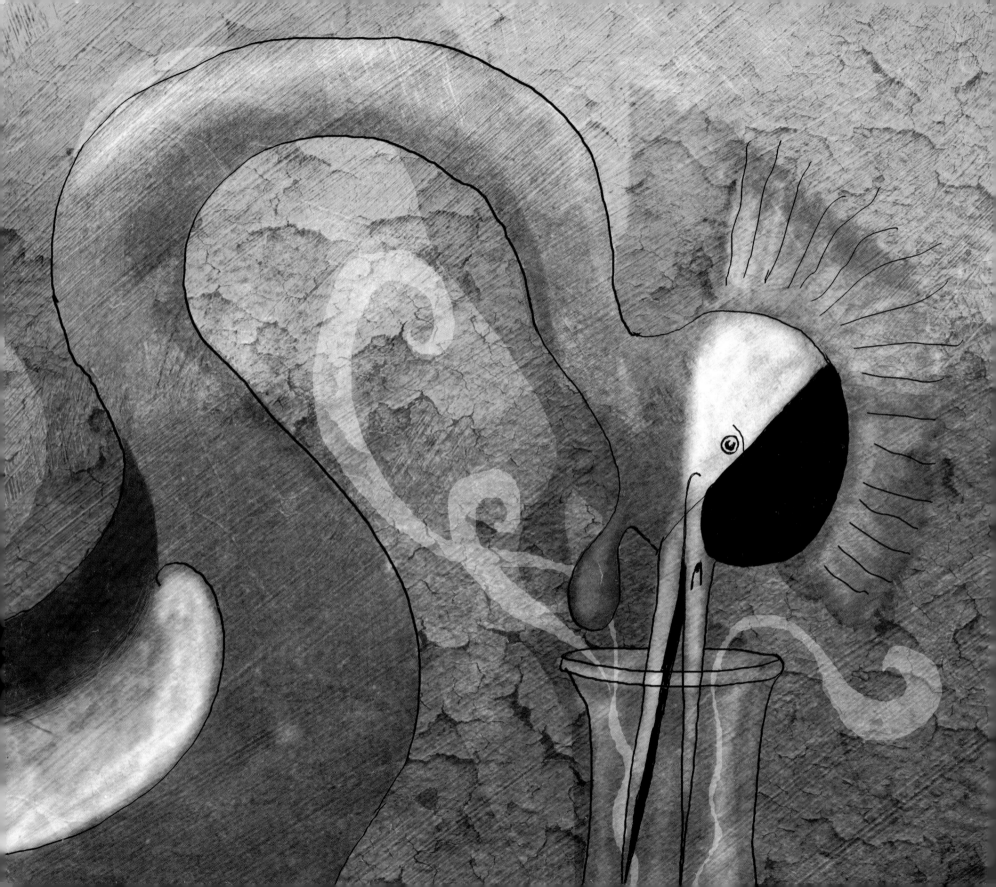

La Grulla tomó su comida muy lentamente, saboreando cada bocado.
"Querido Zorro, muchas gracias por su visita", sonrió, "ha sido un
placer devolverle su amabilidad".

Las tripas del Zorro no cesaban de hacer ruido.
Y cuando se fue a casa, todavía tenía hambre.

Crane ate her meal very slowly, savouring every mouthful.
"Dear Fox, thank you so much for coming," she smiled,
"it has been a pleasure to repay your kindness."

Fox's tummy gurgled and grumbled.
And when he went home, he was still hungry.

The Fox and the Crane

Writing Activity:
Read the story. Explain that we can write our own fable by changing the characters.

Discuss the different animals you could use, bearing in mind what different kinds of dishes they would need! For example, instead of the fox and the crane you could have a tiny mouse and a tall giraffe.

Write an example together as a class, then give the children the opportunity to write their own. Children who need support could be provided with a writing frame.

Art Activity:
Dishes of every colour and kind! Create them from clay, salt dough, play dough… Make them, paint them, decorate them…

Maths Activity:
Provide a variety of vessels: bowls, jugs, vases, mugs… Children can use these to investigate capacity:

Compare the containers and order them from smallest to largest.

Estimate the capacity of each container.

Young children can use non-standard measures e.g. 'about 3 beakers full'.

Check estimates by filling the container with coloured liquid ('soup') or dry lentils.

Older children can use standard measures such as a litre jug, and measure using litres and millilitres. How near were the estimates?

Label each vessel with its capacity.

The King of the Forest

Writing Activity:
Children can write their own fables by changing the setting of this story. Think about what kinds of animals you would find in a different setting. For example how about 'The King of the Arctic' starring an arctic fox and a polar bear!

Storytelling Activity:
Draw a long path down a roll of paper showing the route Fox took through the forest. The children can add their own details, drawing in the various scenes and re-telling the story orally with model animals.

If you are feeling ambitious you could chalk the path onto the playground so that children can act out the story using appropriate noises and movements! (They could even make masks to wear, decorated with feathers, woollen fur, sequin scales etc.)

Music Activity:
Children choose a forest animal. Then select an instrument that will make a sound that matches the way their animal looks and moves. Encourage children to think about musical features such as volume, pitch and rhythm. For example a loud, low, plodding rhythm played on a drum could represent an elephant.

Children perform their animal sounds. Can the class guess the animal?

Children can play their pieces in groups, to create a forest soundscape.

El Rey del Bosque
Una Fábula China

The King of the Forest
A Chinese Fable

retold by Dawn Casey

illustrated by Jago

Spanish translation by
Marta Belén Sáez Cabero

El Zorro estaba paseando por el bosque cuando oyó algo
moverse entre la alta hierba. Y notó…

UN CRUJIDO *Algo grande.*
UN PARPADEO *Algo con ojos amarillos.*
UN DESTELLO *Algo con dientes como cuchillos.*

Fox was walking in the forest when he heard something moving
in the long grass.

RUSTLE Something big.
BLINK Something with yellow eyes.
FLASH Something with teeth like knives.

"Buenos días, zorrito", dijo el Tigre con una sonrisa burlona y una boca llena de dientes.
El Zorro tragó saliva.
"Es un placer conocerte", ronroneó el Tigre, "ya empezaba a tener hambre".
Al Zorro se le ocurrió algo. "¡Cómo te atreves!", dijo. "¿No sabes que soy el Rey del Bosque?"
"¡Tú! ¿El Rey del Bosque?", dijo el Tigre en medio de grandes carcajadas.
"Si no me crees", contestó el Zorro con dignidad, "camina detrás de mí y ya verás. Todos me tienen miedo".
"Eso lo tengo que ver", dijo el Tigre.
Así que el Zorro se puso a andar por el bosque. El Tigre le seguía orgullosamente, con el rabo en alto, hasta que…

"Good morning little fox," Tiger grinned, and his mouth was nothing but teeth.
Fox gulped.
"I am pleased to meet you," Tiger purred. "I was just beginning to feel hungry."
Fox thought fast. "How dare you!" he said. "Don't you know I'm the King of the Forest?"
"You! King of the Forest?" said Tiger, and he roared with laughter.
"If you don't believe me," replied Fox with dignity, "walk behind me and you'll see – everyone is scared of me."
"This I've got to see," said Tiger.
So Fox strolled through the forest. Tiger followed behind proudly, with his tail held high, until…

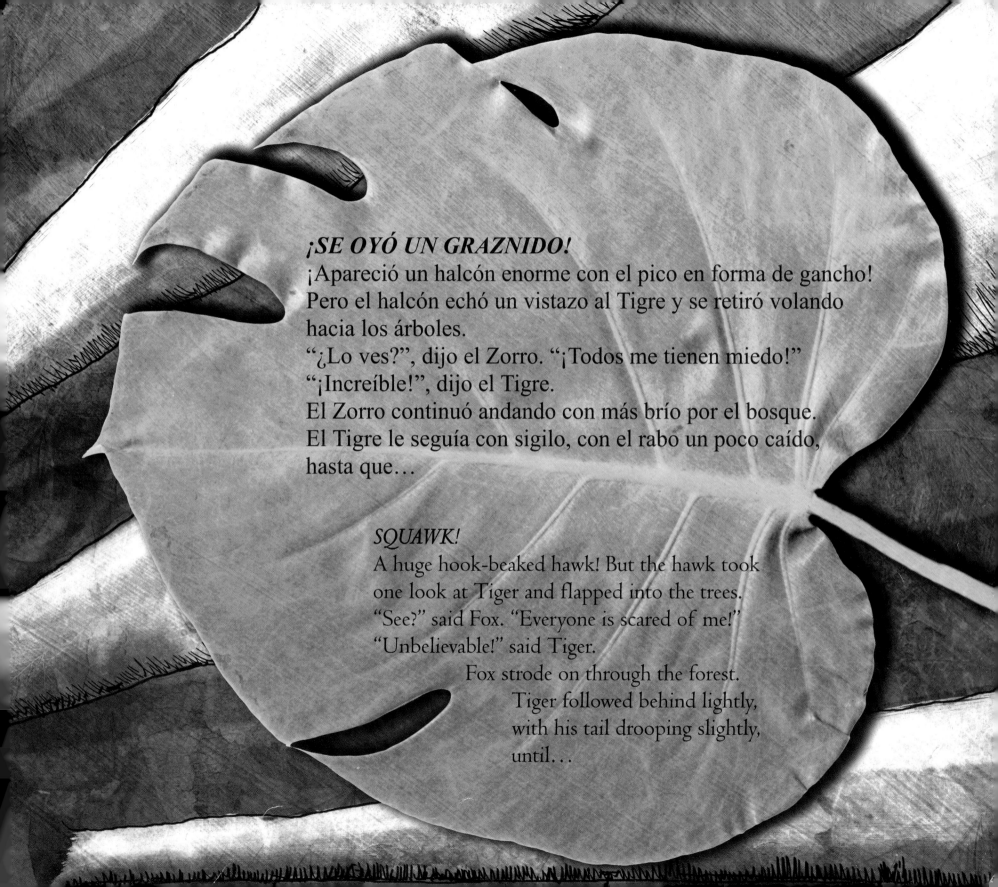

¡SE OYÓ UN GRAZNIDO!
¡Apareció un halcón enorme con el pico en forma de gancho!
Pero el halcón echó un vistazo al Tigre y se retiró volando
hacia los árboles.
"¿Lo ves?", dijo el Zorro. "¡Todos me tienen miedo!"
"¡Increíble!", dijo el Tigre.
El Zorro continuó andando con más brío por el bosque.
El Tigre le seguía con sigilo, con el rabo un poco caído,
hasta que…

SQUAWK!

A huge hook-beaked hawk! But the hawk took
one look at Tiger and flapped into the trees.
"See?" said Fox. "Everyone is scared of me!"
"Unbelievable!" said Tiger.
Fox strode on through the forest.
Tiger followed behind lightly,
with his tail drooping slightly,
until…

¡SE OYÓ UN GRUÑIDO!

¡Apareció un gran oso negro! Pero el oso echó un vistazo
al Tigre y se escondió rápidamente entre los arbustos.
"¿Lo ves?", dijo el Zorro. "¡Todos me tienen miedo!"
"¡Increíble!", dijo el Tigre.
El Zorro prosiguió su caminata por el bosque. El Tigre
le seguía humildemente, arrastrando el rabo por el suelo,
hasta que…

GROWL!

A big black bear! But the bear took one look
at Tiger and crashed into the bushes.
"See?" said Fox. "Everyone is scared of me!"
"Incredible!" said Tiger.
Fox marched on through the forest. Tiger
followed behind meekly, with his tail
dragging on the forest floor, until…

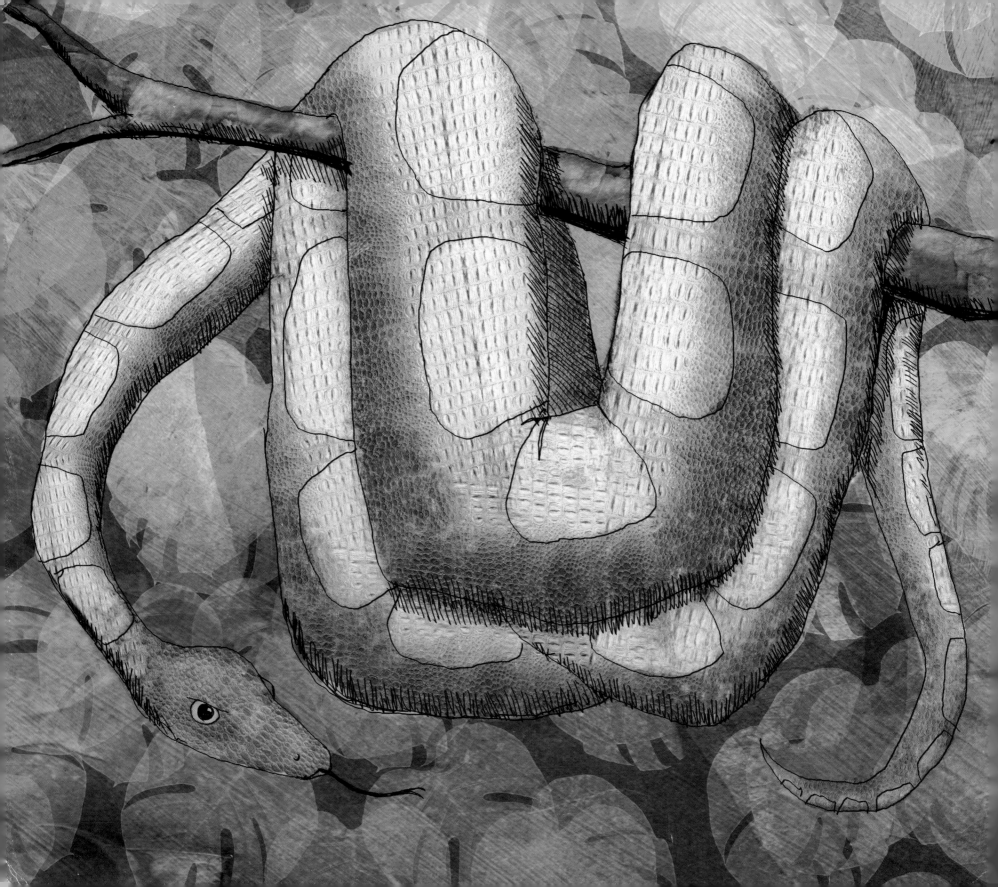

¡SE OYÓ UN SISEO!
¡Apareció una sigilosa y escurridiza serpiente! Pero la serpiente
echó un vistazo al Tigre y se deslizó entre la maleza.
"¿LO VES?", dijo el Zorro. "¡TODOS ME TIENEN MIEDO!"

HISSSSSSS!
A slinky slidey snake! But the snake took one look
at Tiger and slithered into the undergrowth.
"SEE?" said Fox. "EVERYONE IS SCARED
OF ME!"

"Ya lo veo", dijo el Tigre, "eres el Rey del Bosque y yo soy tu humilde servidor".
"Bien", dijo el Zorro. "Entonces, ¡retírate!"

Y el Tigre se fue, con el rabo entre las patas.

"I do see," said Tiger, "you are the King of the Forest and I am your humble servant."
"Good," said Fox. "Then, be gone!"

And Tiger went, with his tail between his legs.

"El Rey del Bosque", pensó el Zorro y sonrió. Su sonrisa se hizo cada vez más amplia, y se convirtió en una risilla tonta, y el Zorro se fue a casa riéndose a carcajadas.

"King of the Forest," said Fox to himself with a smile. His smile grew into a grin, and his grin grew into a giggle, and Fox laughed out loud all the way home.

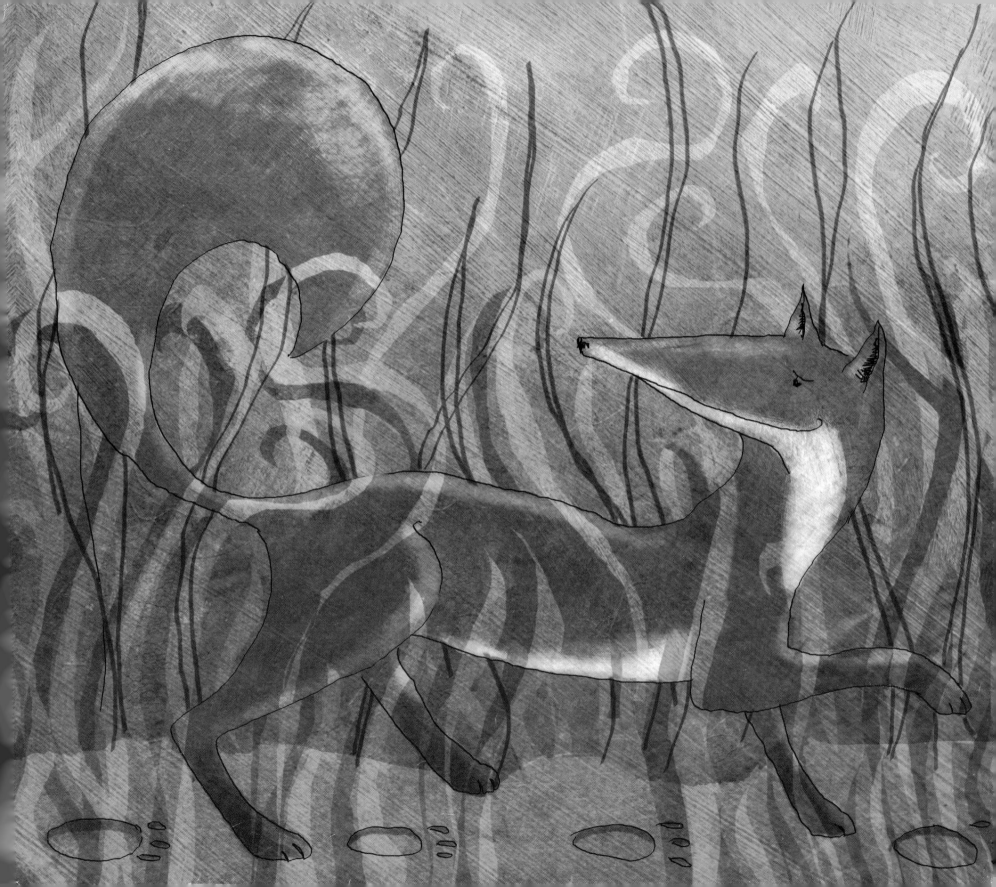

To my Nana, with love ~ DC

For my wife, Alex ~ J

First published in 2006 by Mantra Lingua Ltd
Global House, 303 Ballards Lane
London N12 8NP
www.mantralingua.com

A CIP record for this book is available from the British Library